By **Kelly DiPucchio**  Illustrations by **Mary Lundquist**

# *one* little
# *two* little
# *three* little
# children

BALZER + BRAY
*An Imprint of* HarperCollins*Publishers*

One little,

two little,

three little children.

Loved little,
hugged little,
snugged little children.

Cry little,
shy little,
my little children.

All children

'round the world.

One loving,
two loving,
three loving daddies.

Smart loving,
art-loving,
heart-loving daddies.

Peace-loving,

strong-loving,

long-loving daddies.

All daddies 'round the world.

One playful,

two playful,

three playful mommies.

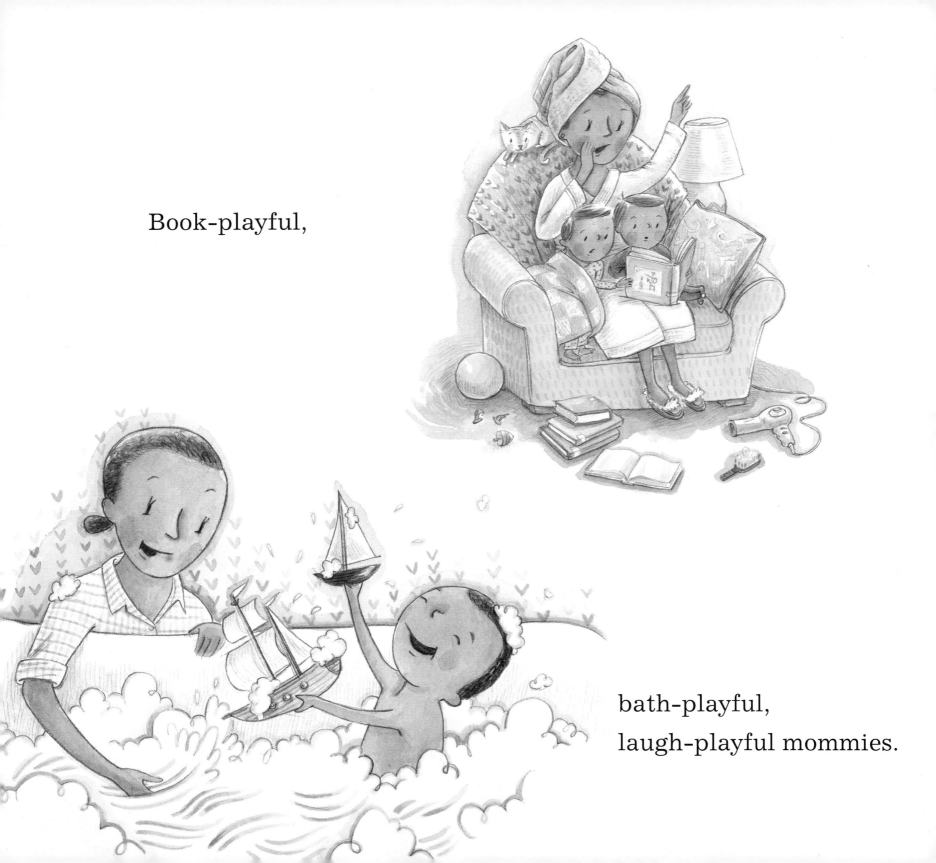

Book-playful,

bath-playful,
laugh-playful mommies.

Rise-playful,

wise-playful,
eyes-playful mommies.

All mommies 'round the world.

One cozy,

two cozy,

three cozy houses.

Big-cozy,

small-cozy,

tall-cozy houses.

Snow-cozy,

stick-cozy,

brick-cozy houses.

All houses

'round the world.

One singing,

two singing,

three singing voices.

Lap-singing, loud-singing, proud-singing voices.

Girl-singing, boy-singing, joy-singing voices.

All voices 'round the world.

Ten little,     nine little,     eight little families.

Furred little,

finned little,
grinned little families.

Kissed little,

kind little,
mine little families . . .

... one BIG family 'round the world.

*For Sylvie*
*—K.D.*

*For Eric*
*—M.L.*

Balzer + Bray is an imprint of HarperCollins Publishers.

One Little Two Little Three Little Children
Text copyright © 2016 by Kelly DiPucchio. Illustrations copyright © 2016 by Mary Lundquist.

Library of Congress Cataloging-in-Publication Data
DiPucchio, Kelly S.
 One little two little three little children / by Kelly DiPucchio ; illustrations by Mary Lundquist. — First edition.
   pages  cm
 Summary: A rhyming celebration of the diversity and universality of children and their families.
 ISBN 978-0-06-234866-1 (hardcover)
 [1. Stories in rhyme. 2. Families—Fiction. 3. Multiculturalism—Fiction.]  I. Lundquist, Mary, illustrator. II. Title.
 PZ8.3.D5998One 2016                                                                                          2014041060
 [E]—dc23                                                                                                              CIP
                                                                                                                        AC

The artist used pencil and watercolor on watercolor paper to create the illustrations for this book.
Typography by Dana Fritts
15  16  17  18  19   SCP   10 9 8 7 6 5 4 3 2 1
❖ First Edition